Fraser

Written by Chantal Henry-Biabaud
Illustrated by Bernard Dagan

Specialist Adviser:
*Solange Magalhaës
Brazilian Ministry of Culture*

*ISBN 0-944589-28-6
First U.S. Publication 1991 by
Young Discovery Library
217 Main St. • Ossining, NY 10562*

YOUNG DISCOVERY LIBRARY

Living in
South America

YOUNG DISCOVERY LIBRARY

Do you know the history of South America?

Its first inhabitants were Indians. One group, the Incas, had a splendid empire with cities, roads and canals. In the early 16th century, sailors from Spain and Portugal crossed the wide Atlantic Ocean. These daring explorers sailed in ships called *caravels.**

*Reader, please note: we have put most of the Indian, Spanish and Portugese words in *italic.* This is to indicate it is a foreign word.

The Incas of Peru believed that their emperor was descended from the Sun, the supreme god.

The explorers became **known as conquistadors.** They found a continent unknown to other Europeans. They conquered vast lands in Peru and Brazil, ending the Incas' Empire. Most Indians were forced into slavery or killed. Many more Europeans came to live in South America. They brought Africans for use as slaves too. Today, Spanish is the main language in South America. The exception is Brazil, where Portugese is used.

The Incas made many objects from baked clay, called *terra cotta.* Their golden statuettes were much desired by the Europeans.

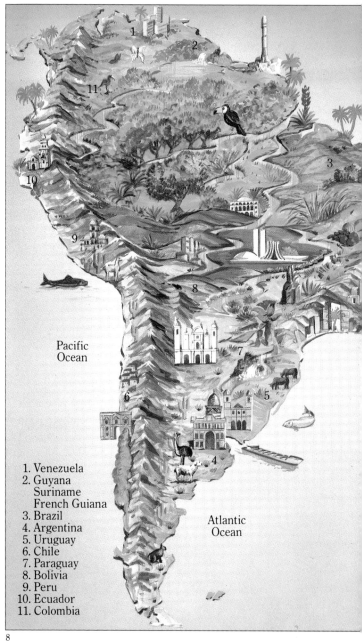

Pacific
Ocean

Atlantic
Ocean

1. Venezuela
2. Guyana
   Suriname
   French Guiana
3. Brazil
4. Argentina
5. Uruguay
6. Chile
7. Paraguay
8. Bolivia
9. Peru
10. Ecuador
11. Colombia

Let's discover this vast continent!

To the west, the Andes *cordillera,* or mountain range, lifts its snowcapped peaks to the sky.

In the center is an enormous forest covering half of Brazil—the **Amazon jungle.** Flowing through it is the Amazon River, carrying more water than any river in the world! The Pacific coast is dry while much of the Atlantic side is green and has more people.

Way down south, below the tableland region of **Patagonia,** is *Tierra del Fuego* or "land of fire." It is an island group with land like the surface of the moon! Not a single tree grows there, and high winds constantly blow. A hard place to live in.

In all, there are thirteen countries in South America. Brazil alone takes up half of the continent.

Very long ago,
South America and Africa
were a single continent,
which broke in two and
drifted apart.

The Altiplano is the land of the llama and the condor.

High plateaus and tropical beaches

At the foot of the Andes lies the *altiplano,* or highlands, at an altitude of between 10,000 and 15,000 feet. This is where the mountain Indians live. On the north side of the continent stretch the fine, sandy beaches of Venezuela's Caribbean coast.

The clear water is alive with colorful fish.

Here are some of the most out-of-the-way peaks in the world.

At the border between Chile and Argentina, you can see the peaks of the Andes and the glaciers which melt to feed Argentinian lakes. Near the tip of the continent is Ushuaia, farthest-south city in the world. Last is **Cape Horn**, a fearsome place to sail. Many ships have been lost in its stormy seas.

At Cape Horn, where winds often reach 120 mph, the waves are very dangerous.

To get to Cuzco, one of the world's highest cities, you can take a train which climbs to 11,000 feet above sea level. If you are not used to it, the thin air will make you dizzy and out-of-breath. Cuzco, in the heart of the Andes, was once the capital of the Inca Empire. It was called "City of the Sun" and attracts many tourists today. Women come from faraway villages to sell vegetables and poultry at the market. Others sell mango, guava or banana juice on the street corners. The days are sunny and the nights are very cool.

Many of the buildings are hundreds of years old.

These Incan walls were so well built—without mortar—you can hardly fit a needle between the stones!

13

Every tribe of the Andes has its own customs, traditions and dress.
The women wear layers of colorful skirts with the oldest one underneath. They weave their own large woolen shawls. You can tell the tribes apart by looking at the women's hats. Meals are often eaten outside. **Spicy dishes contain tomatoes, potatoes and corn**—this is where those vegetables come from! Brought back to Europe corn and potatoes proved as valuable as gold. Easy to grow, they freed millions of people for factory work.

Gauchos (cowboys) herd cattle in the hill country.

Indians travel enormous distances from their farms to the marketplaces in town. Some have replaced their llamas with horses and mules which were once brought to their lands by the Spaniards.
A horse or mule can not only carry a pack, it can carry the farmer, too!

After selling their goods at the market, the men eat a big meal before starting the long journey back to their farms.

If you flew over South America at the equator, you would see nothing but green. **This is the immense Amazon jungle** covering hundreds of thousands of square miles! An enormous river, also called the Amazon, snakes its way through the jungle. It starts high in the snowcapped peaks of Peru and winds 4,200 miles through Brazil to the sea.

The Amazon is the place for gold-seekers, rubber harvesters and a few remaining Indian tribes: the Yanomami, Jivaros and Matis.

The forest holds no secrets for the Indians, who are skillful hunters and fishermen. The Brazilian government is trying to keep ranchers from clearing Indian lands for cattle raising.

The slow-moving sloth lives in the treetops. He spends most of his time hanging upside down!

It is very quiet when you walk in the Amazon jungle. But don't think that you are alone! You cannot sit down for a moment without being bitten by ants or mosquitos. What looks like a flower is really a clump of butterflies—up they fly! In the treetops, as high as a ten-story building, lives a whole world of animals.

Birds and insects flit about, monkeys screech and snakes are on the hunt for food.

The anaconda is one of the world's largest snakes. It kills its prey by spueezing it to death.

There are parrots of all kinds, toucans
with their big beaks, howler monkeys
and monkeys no bigger than your hand.
The river is teeming with crocodiles,
piranhas and giant fish.

There are over a million kinds of insects, ticks, flies and mosquitos
to make your life miserable in the jungle! The piranha's teeth are
so sharp the Indians use them as razor blades.

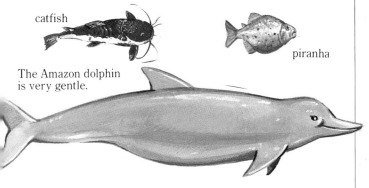

catfish

piranha

The Amazon dolphin
is very gentle.

But at least you won't die of hunger.
There are pineapples, avocados, nuts and
passionfruit.

Here and there along the river, you can see an isolated house. This is where the **caboclos**, or jungle-dwellers, live. When a boat goes by, they come out and wave. They build their houses on pilings because the river rises during the rainy season. They don't need cars or bicycles because there are no roads! Everyone travels by *piragua*, or dugout canoe, on the river.

Children often have monkeys as pets. These little friends also groom their owner's hair.

The piragua is used for fishing, carrying supplies and for fun. Children go for canoe rides instead of bike rides. They learn to handle a piragua when very young.

On the northern coast of Brazil
there is a dry region called the
Sertão. It has beautiful, long
white beaches.
On this coast, fishing is a main
industry. Two or three fishermen
sail standing up, using a paddle
to steer. They can keep their
balance even in very high waves.
Every evening they bring the boats
ashore, often using logs as
rollers.

As soon as the catch is brought ashore,
it is taken to be sold.

This Brazilian woman needs both skill and patience to create a sand scene in a bottle!

The natives of this region are very clever at handicrafts.

Further back in the dunes, you can find many different colors of sand. Some artists carefully pour the sand into bottles of various shapes and sizes to create striking landscapes. Once, only the pale, natural colors were used, but today, brightly dyed sand often fills the bottles.

Scoop up a few bucketfuls of different colored sand, find a pretty bottle and a thin spatula, and try your luck at a "sandscape"!

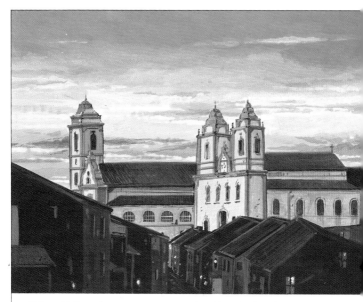

It is said that there are as many churches in the city of Salvador as there are days in the year.

The citizens of Salvador are devout Catholics who often take part in processions with flower-covered statues of saints.

In Salvador, in the state of Bahia, you can relive Brazil's history.
Here the Portugese tried to capture the Indians and make them work on sugar plantations. But the Indians preferred to fight, and even die, rather than be slaves. The Portugese then brought black slaves from Africa. Because they were in a strange land, far from their tribal homes, these slaves were easier to control.

Today there are no more slaves. The people have a mixed heritage from Europe, Africa and the original Indians. On the streets of Bahia you see women dressed in white lace with colorful necklaces and turbans. The favorite foods are cooked in big pots... spicy dishes of coconut milk, lime juice, shrimp and red pepper.

Sometimes you can see a demonstration of *capoeira*, an exciting dance like slow-motion wrestling.

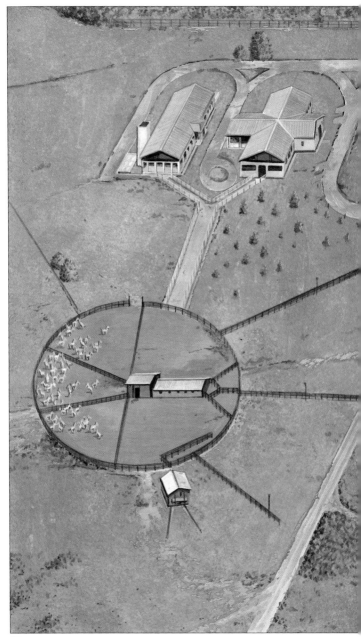

26

Southern Brazil is very different.
Like Argentina next door, it is a
land of sheep and cattle, gauchos and
big ranches. These huge ranches are
fazendas in Brazil and *haciendas* in
Argentina. Gauchos there seem to live
in the saddle. They lasso cattle and
work very like North American cowboys.
The ranch people are big meat-eaters.
They love large pieces of meat grilled
on a barbecue and sliced right onto
a plate in thin strips. Lamb, pork
and chicken are all used but the
favorite *carne* (meat) is beef.
These people are very independent
and do not like a lot of laws. Gaucho
"armies" often fought the government
in the past.

The grassy plains are called *pampas.* Out
there you will see gauchos grilling meat.

Rio de Janeiro, or "river of January" is the name of a river which never existed. The first navigators saw the vast bay and thought it was the mouth of a river! The famous beaches of Rio—Ipanema, Copacabana, Leblon—stretch along the coast for miles.

The coast is dotted by peaks with names like Sugarloaf and Hunchback. On one a colossal statue of Christ watches over the *Cariocas*, as the people of Rio are known. Rio is one of the most beautiful cities in the world. It is big, noisy and always busy. Crowds fill the sidewalks and traffic covers the streets.

The calvalcade is a long road of colorful tiles following the beaches. It is used by joggers, bikers and strollers.

You can buy an ice pop or a cool tea with lemon and many other things on the beach.

Children go to school only in the morning because the afternoons are too hot. Every school has its own uniform and a bus which picks up the children outside their homes. But the most important place to be is the beach. Everyone loves to meet there, and Cariocas will use any excuse to go!

No one is allowed to touch these sacred *macumbas* lit for the goddess of the sea.

Swimming is tricky because the waves are so high, and very few people swim out past the breakers. Most beach-goers cool off at the water's edge. Afterwards, everyone gets together for a *feijoada*. It's the national dish, made of black beans and pork, with green cabbage and orange slices on the side. It's a little heavy when the temperature is nearly 100 degrees in the shade, but it is tasty!

Rio's taxi drivers are so reckless that you might feel safer walking!

February in Rio is Carnival time. Everyone enjoys watching the costumed samba dancers.

Most big cities have slums and Rio has some of the worst. On the hillsides are the *favelas* or shantytowns: thousands of tiny, colorful houses with tin roofs. These are the saddest of people. Many are sick due to poor diet and few doctors to help them. Families send their children out to earn a little money, selling candy or lemons on the streets.

The Maracaña is the world's biggest soccer stadium: it can hold 200,000 sports-lovers. That is where Pelé made his 1,000th goal.

34

While Rio is full of beaches and entertainment, **São Paulo, is all business!** It is a bustling city of skyscrapers and criss-crossing highways. There is even an airport right in the middle of town. Unfortunately, São Paulo is also one of the most polluted cities in the world.

Brasilia is the new, ultramodern capital of Brazil. It was built in the wilderness in only four years.

In the 18th century, São Paulo's fortune was built on coffee. The bean grew very well in the area's red soil and there was a fine port to handle shipments to the world. Brazil is the largest coffee producing country. Today, São Paulo shows the best and the worst parts of South America. Wealth and poverty live side by side.

The great falls at Iguacú

The Iguacú River (say ee-gwa-soo) is on the border of Brazil and Argentina. Hundreds of waterfalls, some of them 240 feet high, cascade into a narrow gorge. Just a hundred miles away are the falls at Guaira. Those have a greater flow of water than any other falls in the world.

Index